CONTENTS

The AMAZING ADVENTURES of BATMAN™

BLOSSOM BATTLE!

by **Laurie S. Sutton**
illustrated by **Dario Brizuela**

Batman created by Bob Kane with Bill Finger

Raintree is an imprint of Capstone Global Library Limited, a company incorporated in England and Wales having its registered office at 264 Banbury Road, Oxford, OX2 7DY – Registered company number: 6695582

www.raintree.co.uk
myorders@raintree.co.uk

This edition published for Raintree in 2019.

British Library Cataloguing in Publication Data
A full catalogue record for this book is available from the British Library.
ISBN: 978 1 4747 7452 9

Editor: Christopher Harbo
Designer: Kayla Rossow

Printed and bound in India.

Hidden in the shadows,
a hero keeps watch.
He is the Caped Crusader
against crime. He is the
Dark Knight of justice.
These are ...

The AMAZING ADVENTURES of
BATMAN™

Chapter 1

BLOOMING BLUNDER

FWOOSH!

Batman flies through the night sky in the Batplane. He looks for crime as he soars over old, ruined buildings in Gotham City.

"Those buildings look like good places for criminals to hide," the Dark Knight says. He swoops the Batplane lower for a closer look.

On the ground, Poison

Ivy spots the Batplane flying

overhead. The villain ducks

into one of the buildings.

"I can't let

Batman see me,"

she says.

The building

is a greenhouse

filled with strange plants.

Poison Ivy pats each one of

them like a pet.

"Hello, Sprout. Hello, Spike," she says, greeting each plant by name. "How are you doing today? Are you feeling hungry?"

Poison Ivy pulls out a bottle of experimental plant food. She opens the lid and puts a few drops on some of the potted plants.

PLOP! PLOP! PLOP!

The plant food soaks into the soil. The plants shiver as they suck up the food.

"This plant food will make you big and strong," Ivy says.

The plants grow larger.

Their pots crack.

"See?" Poison Ivy says.

"It's just like taking your

vitamins!"

Suddenly the plants

reach out with their flowers.

They attack Poison Ivy.

"Oh no! Why is this

happening?" Ivy cries.

A giant ivy vine shoots towards the ceiling.

CRAAAASH!

It smashes right through the roof of the greenhouse!

Chapter 2

MUTANT MENACE

In the Batplane, Batman
sees the giant vine burst
from the old building.

"A monster plant!"
Batman says. "Poison Ivy
must be up to something."

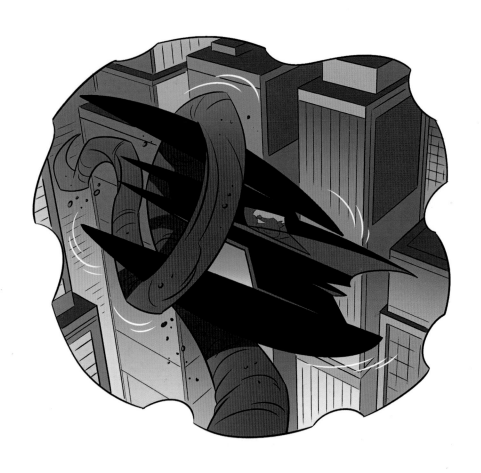

Suddenly the huge vine reaches out and grabs the Batplane. The jet can't break free from the plant's powerful grip.

"I need to call for backup," Batman says. He pushes a button and sends out a call on his radio.

Batgirl is patrolling Gotham City's streets when she gets Batman's call.

"Batgirl, I need your help," the Dark Knight says over the radio.

"I'm on my way!" Batgirl replies. She speeds on her Batcycle to help her friend.

Batgirl arrives in time to see the giant ivy vine crush the Batplane. **SCRUNCH!**

But Batgirl sees Batman eject and spread the wings of a Bat-glider. He swoops through the air as the vine continues to grow.

"There's only one way to get to the root of this problem," Batgirl says.

Batgirl pulls a freeze-gas capsule from her Utility Belt. She throws it at the vine.

KRAAAAKLE!

The giant plant turns to ice. Batman hits it with a Batarang. The vine shatters into pieces.

Chapter 3

FLOWER FAILURE

Inside the greenhouse, huge flowers bloom. They grow up out of the building. Poison Ivy's plant food has turned daisies, tulips and roses into a major menace!

"Help!" Poison Ivy cries, as a huge daisy creeps towards her. "I can't control these plants!" The villain is in danger from her own creations.

Batman and Batgirl burst into the greenhouse. They see Poison Ivy in trouble.

"It looks like we need to save the day . . . and the villain," Batgirl says.

Batman uses a Batrope

to drag the dangerous

daisy away from Poison Ivy.

Batgirl throws a net over a

bunch of twisting tulips.

While the super heroes battle the blossoms, Poison Ivy tries to sneak away.

SWOOOOSH! The Dark Knight tosses a Batrope. It wraps around Poison Ivy.

Batgirl throws two of her Batarangs. **THUNK! THUNK!** They pin the villain to the wall. Then the heroes fling more Batarangs to snip off the flowers.

"Thanks for another really amazing adventure, Batman," says Batgirl.

"I'm just glad we could nip it in the bud," replies the Dark Knight.

BATMAN'S
SECRET MESSAGE!

Hey, kids! What is Poison Ivy's real name?

16 1 13 5 12 1

9 19 12 5 25

Use the code below to solve the Batcomputer's secret message!

1	2	3	4	5	6	7	8	9	10	11	12	13
A	B	C	D	E	F	G	H	I	J	K	L	M

14	15	16	17	18	19	20	21	22	23	24	25	26
N	O	P	Q	R	S	T	U	V	W	X	Y	Z

capsule small container that holds something

experimental to do with something that has not been tested thoroughly

greenhouse warm building where plants can grow

menace threat or danger

patrol to protect and watch an area

villain wicked, evil or bad person in a story

vitamin nutrient that helps keep people healthy

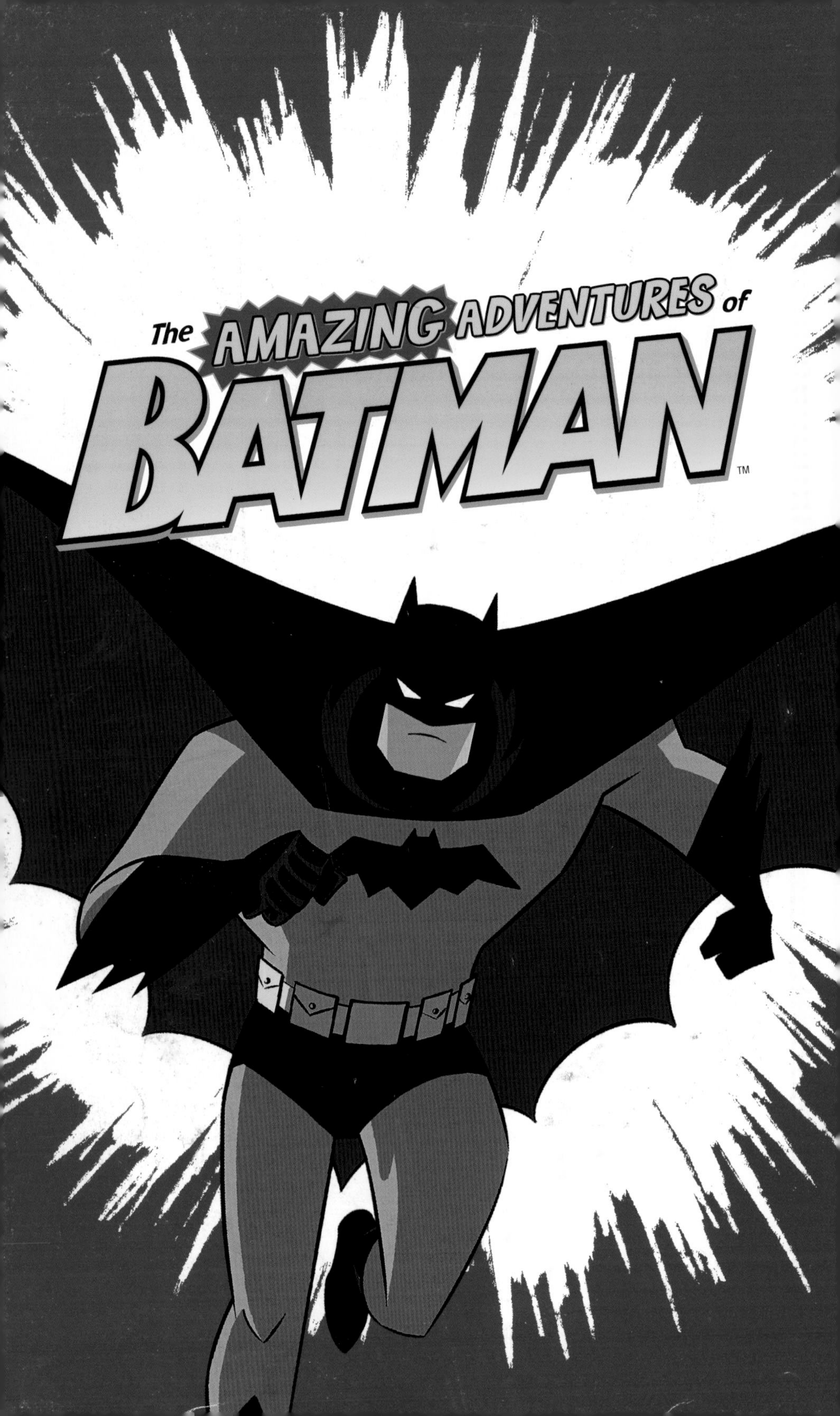
The AMAZING ADVENTURES of
BATMAN™

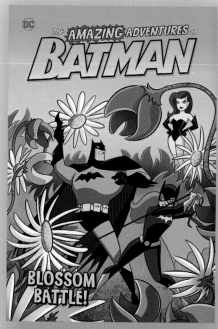

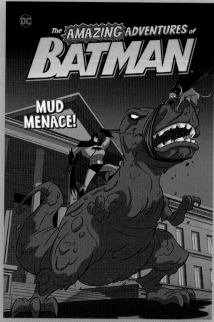

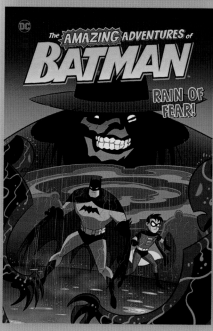

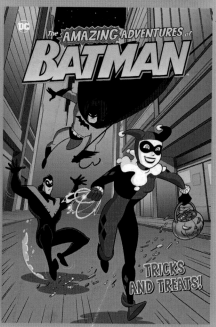

COLLECT THEM ALL!

only from . . . **RAINTREE**

Author

Laurie S. Sutton has read comics since she was a child. She grew up to become an editor for Marvel, DC Comics, Starblaze and Tekno Comics. She has written for series such as Adam Strange for DC, Star Trek: Voyager for Marvel, and Star Trek: Deep Space Nine and Witch Hunter for Malibu Comics. There are long boxes of comics in her wardrobe where there should be clothes and shoes. Laurie has lived all over the world, and currently lives in Florida, USA.

Illustrator

Dario Brizuela was born in Buenos Aires, Argentina, in 1977. He enjoys doing illustration work and character design for several companies including DC Comics, Marvel Comics, Image Comics, IDW Publishing, Titan Publishing, Hasbro, Capstone Publishers and Disney Publishing Worldwide. Dario's work can be found in a wide range of creations, including Star Wars Tales, Ben 10, DC Super Friends, Justice League Unlimited, Batman: The Brave & The Bold, Transformers, Teenage Mutant Ninja Turtles, Batman 66, Wonder Woman 77, Teen Titans Go!, Scooby Doo! Team Up and DC Super Hero Girls.